MW00884784

# Roll Tide™!

## Kenny Stabler

### Illustrated by Miguel De Angel

MASCOT BOOKS

www.mascotbooks.com

It was Homecoming at the University of Alabama. Big Al joined his friends on the Quad for the traditional bonfire.

Alabama fans cheered, "Roll Tide!"

The next morning, Big Al joined the Homecoming Parade. He was happy to see so many Bama fans back in Tuscaloosa.

Big Al waved to his fans as the crowd cheered, "Roll Tide!"

Big Al headed to the Quad where he found the delicious smell of southern cooking too much to resist.

A group of fans gathered around the
grill and cheered, "Roll Tide!"

After enjoying a big meal, Big Al played
on the Quad with some children.

As they played, the children cheered,
"Roll Tide!"

Inside the bookstore,
Big Al ran into Alabama fans buying
Crimson Tide souvenirs.

The bookstore worker cheered,
"Roll Tide!"

1992 National
Championship Trophy

At the Bear Bryant Museum,
Big Al admired Alabama's
championship tradition.

Coach Bryant's houndstooth hat.

Outside the Museum, Big Al
hugged a group of children.
The children cheered, "Roll Tide!"

Big Al met the football team
in the locker room before the start
of the big game.

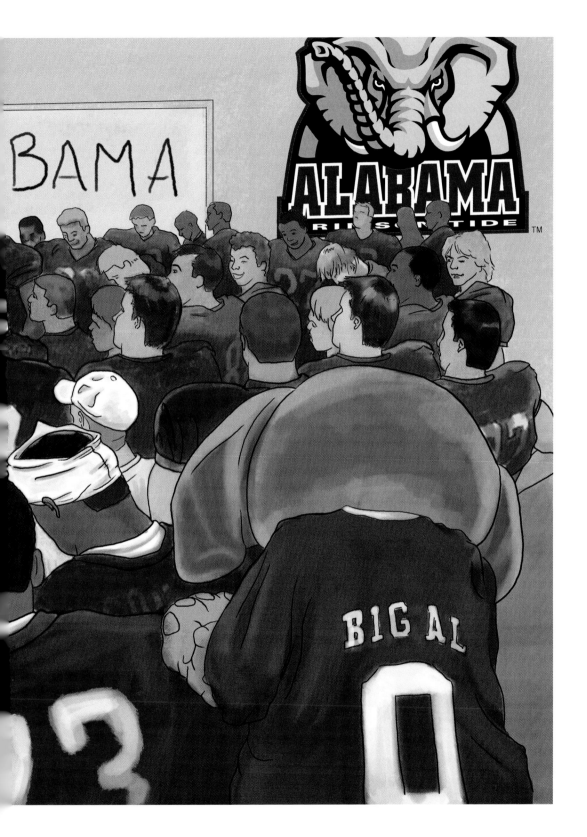

The coach encouraged the team
to play Alabama Football.
The team cheered, "Roll Tide!"

Big Al and the cheerleaders ran
onto the field. The Crimson Tide
football team followed.

"This is Alabama Football!"
called the stadium announcer.
The crowd cheered, "Roll Tide!"

The Crimson Tide scored
four touchdowns in the first half!

The cheerleaders cheered, "Roll Tide!"

The famous Million Dollar Band performed at halftime. They marched into formation and played, "Yea Alabama!"

As the band played,
the crowd cheered, "Roll Tide!"

Alabama won the football game!
The players dumped water on the
coach to celebrate the victory.

The team threw Big Al high into the air.
Big Al cheered, "Roll Tide!"

For Jack and Justin. - Kenny Stabler

For Sue, Ana Milagros, and Angel Miguel ~ Miguel De Angel

For more information about our products,
please visit us online at www.mascotbooks.com.

Copyright © 2006, Mascot Books, Inc.  All rights reserved.
No part of this book may be reproduced by any means.

For more information, please contact Mascot Books,
P.O. Box 220157, Chantilly, VA 20153-0157

BIG AL, UNIVERSITY OF ALABAMA, CRIMSON TIDE,
BAMA, and ROLL TIDE, are trademarks or
registered trademarks of The University of Alabama.

ISBN: 1-932888-48-9

Printed in the United States.

www.mascotbooks.com